THE DINOSAUR

Tim Collins

Illustrated by James Lawrence

Titles in Monster Island:

THE APE
TIM COLLINS & ABBY RYDER

THE DINOSAUR
TIM COLLINS & JAMES LAWRENCE

THE SQUID
TIM COLLINS & JAMES LAWRENCE

THE YETI
TIM COLLINS & ABBY RYDER

THE CRAB
TIM COLLINS & JAMES LAWRENCE

THE CYCLOPS
TIM COLLINS & ABBY RYDER

Badger Publishing Limited, Oldmedow Road,
Hardwick Industrial Estate, King's Lynn PE30 4JJ

Telephone: 01438 791037
www.badgerlearning.co.uk

The Dinosaur ISBN 978-1-78837-349-4

2 4 6 8 10 9 7 5 3 1

Publisher: Senior Editor: Danny Pearson
Editor: Claire Morgan
Dee Reid
Designer: Fiona Grant
Cover Illustration: Mark Penman
Illustration: James Lawrence

THE DINOSAUR

Tim Collins

Illustrated by James Lawrence

Contents

Badger
L E A R N I N G

Story Vocabulary
escape
huge
pouring

The story so far...

Scott and Jess were stuck on the island.

They came to a high stone wall.

"Welcome to Monster Island," said a man. "I am the Captain. You should not climb over the wall."

Scott and Jess laughed. They thought the Captain was crazy.

"Why is it called Monster Island?" asked Jess.

"You will soon find out," said the Captain.

Chapter 1

The Wall

"Let's climb the wall," said Scott. "Maybe we will find a way to escape from the island."

"Maybe the wall was built to keep something in," said Jess.

"Well, I'm going to see what is on the other side," said Scott.

Just then, Scott and Jess heard the Captain laughing.

"You are making a big mistake," he said.

"We will see!" said Scott, and he began
to climb the wall.

Jess didn't want to be left with the
Captain so she began to climb too.

When they got to the top of the wall
they used a vine to climb down.

But when they got to the bottom,
the vine fell to the ground.

This side of the wall was slippy.

There was no way to climb back over.

Scott and Jess walked up a hill.

"Can you feel the ground shaking?"
asked Scott.

"Yes!" said Jess.

Then they heard a loud roar.

A huge dinosaur was charging at them,
making the ground shake.

Chapter 2

Attack

"Keep still," shouted Scott. "The dinosaur will only attack us if we move. If we keep still, it won't know we are here."

Jess looked back at the wall.

If they ran now they could get to the wall before the dinosaur got to them.

The Captain had climbed to the top of the wall.

He shouted at Scott and Jess, "Run for your lives!"

"No! Keep still," said Scott. "Then the dinosaur won't see us."

The dinosaur was getting closer and closer.

Jess didn't know what to do.

"I think it can see us," said Jess.
"We need to go!"

"The Captain is just trying to trick us,"
said Scott. "I'm staying here."

"Well, I'm not!" said Jess.

As she ran to the wall she heard Scott scream.

She turned back to look.

The dinosaur's huge teeth were ripping into Scott's chest.

Blood was pouring out.

Chapter 3

Rescue

Jess tried to climb the wall, but she couldn't.

It was too flat and slippy.

She was stuck.

She looked back.

The dinosaur was charging at her.

Its teeth and claws were dripping with Scott's blood.

"Help!" screamed Jess.

Suddenly, a rope was thrown over the wall.

Jess grabbed the rope and began to climb up.

The dinosaur's huge teeth were snapping at her legs.

Jess's arms and legs were getting tired.

I'm going to die, she thought.

She felt the dinosaur's teeth rip her skin.

Then her fingers felt the top of the wall.

Jess pulled herself up and then climbed down the rough side of the wall to the ground.

She could hear the dinosaur crashing into the other side of the wall, but it couldn't get over.

She was safe.

"Thank you," said Jess.

But there was no one there.

She had got away from the dinosaur but her leg was pouring with blood and she was stuck on the island all on her own.

Ape Mountain

Yeti Cave

Crab Cove

Dinosaur Pen

Cyclops Forest

Squid Sea

SQUID INK

Questions

Chapter 1

Why does Scott want to climb over the wall? *(page 6)*

What does the Captain tell them? *(page 8)*

Chapter 2

Why does Scott want to keep still?
(page 14)

What can Jess hear behind her as she runs to the wall? *(page 18)*

Chapter 3

What gets thrown over the wall? *(page 24)*

Where do you think the Captain has gone?

About the Author
Tim Collins has written over 70 books for children and adults.

He lives near Oxford and spends his time listening to rock music and playing Pokémon.

He went to a real desert island once, but he didn't see any monsters.

About the Illustrator
James Lawrence loves reading comic books.

He lives in Manchester and he spends his days drawing cool pictures.

He thinks he could be friends with the Captain.

Hi Lo

3 8002 01796 822 5